KEAN SOO

MARCH GRAND PRIX

THE GREAT DESERT RALLY

STONE ARCH BOOKS
a capstone imprint

March Grand Prix
published by Stone Arch Books,
a Capstone Imprint
1710 Roe Crest Drive
North Mankato, Minnesota 56003
www.capstonepub.com

Cataloging-in-Publication Data is available on
the Library of Congress website.

ISBN: 978-1-4342-9641-2 (library hardcover)
ISBN: 978-1-4342-9644-3 (paperback)
ISBN: 978-1-4965-0186-8 (eBook)

Summary: A new, turbo-charged graphic novel
by Kean Soo, author of the acclaimed, award-
winning series Jellaby. March Hare wants to be
the fastest and furriest race car driver around.
But first, this rabbit racer will have to prove his
skill at the speedway, on the streets, and in the
desert. With pedal-to-the-metal illustrations and
full-throttle action, March is sure to be a winner!

Printed in China by Nordica.
0415/CA21500596
042015   008843NORDF15

To Tory,

For being the best co-driver I could ever ask for.

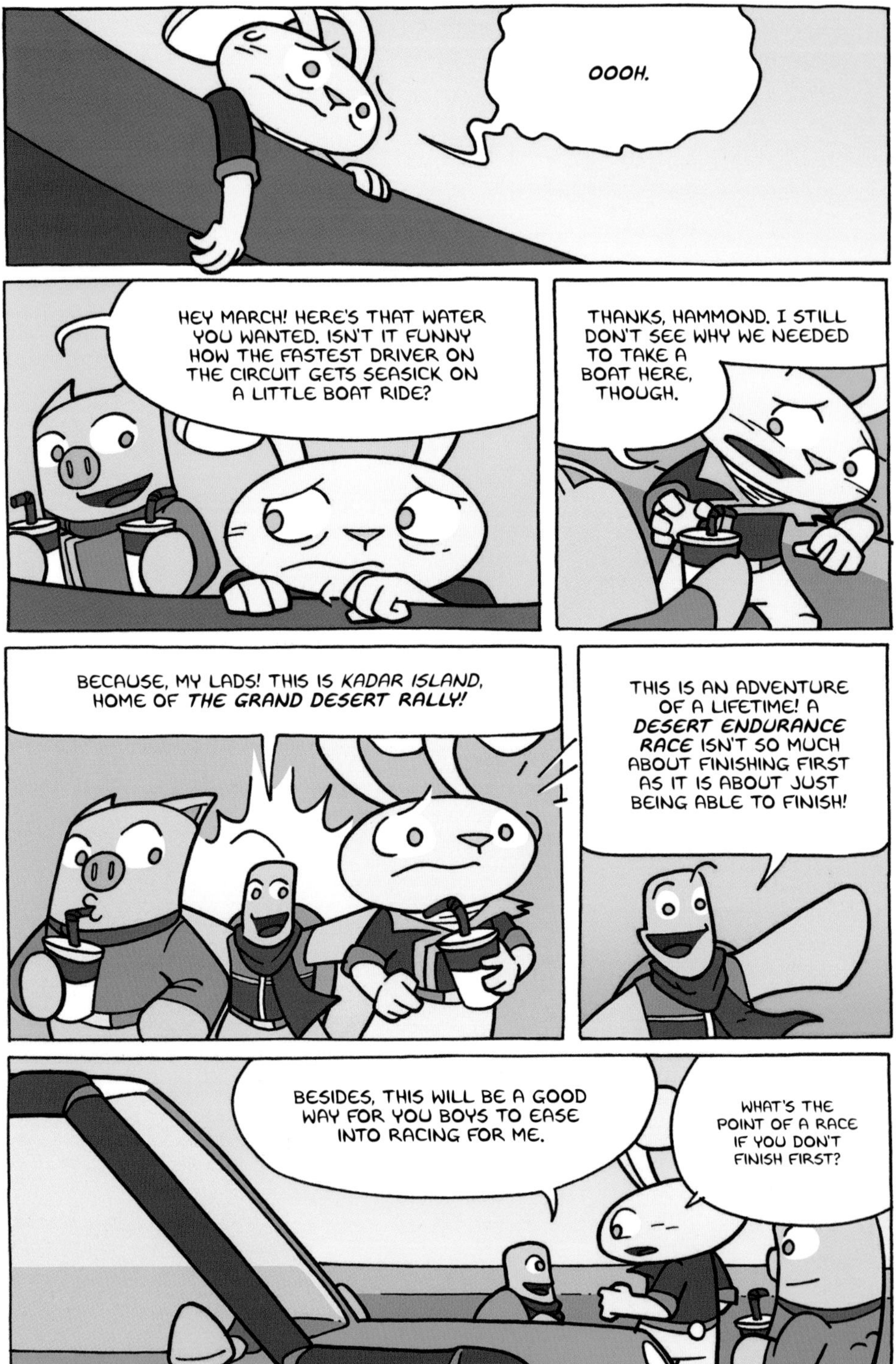
OOOH.
HEY MARCH! HERE'S THAT WATER YOU WANTED. ISN'T IT FUNNY HOW THE FASTEST DRIVER ON THE CIRCUIT GETS SEASICK ON A LITTLE BOAT RIDE?
THANKS, HAMMOND. I STILL DON'T SEE WHY WE NEEDED TO TAKE A BOAT HERE, THOUGH.
BECAUSE, MY LADS! THIS IS *KADAR ISLAND*, HOME OF *THE GRAND DESERT RALLY!*
THIS IS AN ADVENTURE OF A LIFETIME! A *DESERT ENDURANCE RACE* ISN'T SO MUCH ABOUT FINISHING FIRST AS IT IS ABOUT JUST BEING ABLE TO FINISH!
BESIDES, THIS WILL BE A GOOD WAY FOR YOU BOYS TO EASE INTO RACING FOR ME.
WHAT'S THE POINT OF A RACE IF YOU DON'T FINISH FIRST?

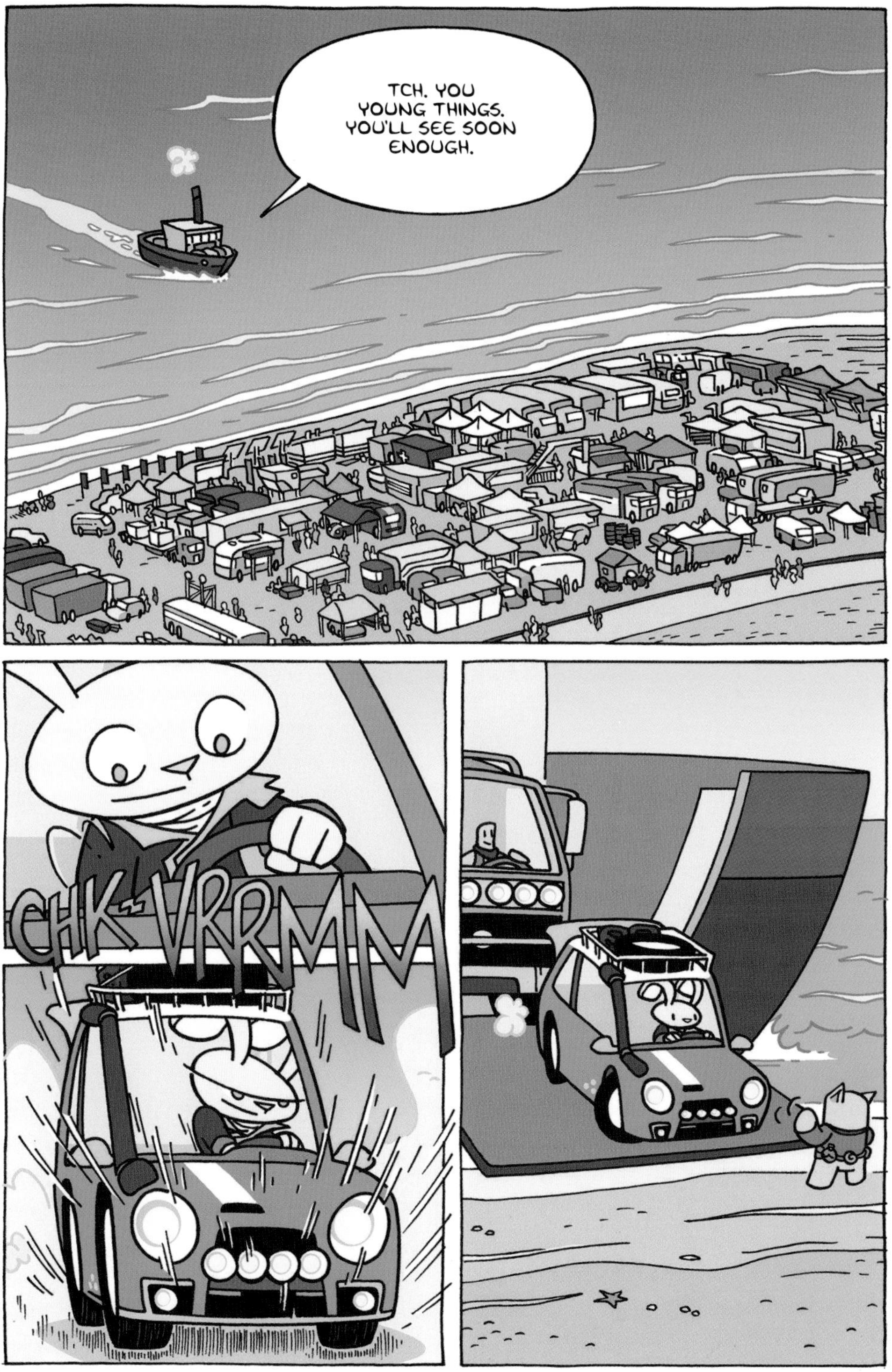
TCH. YOU YOUNG THINGS. YOU'LL SEE SOON ENOUGH.
CHK-VRRMMM

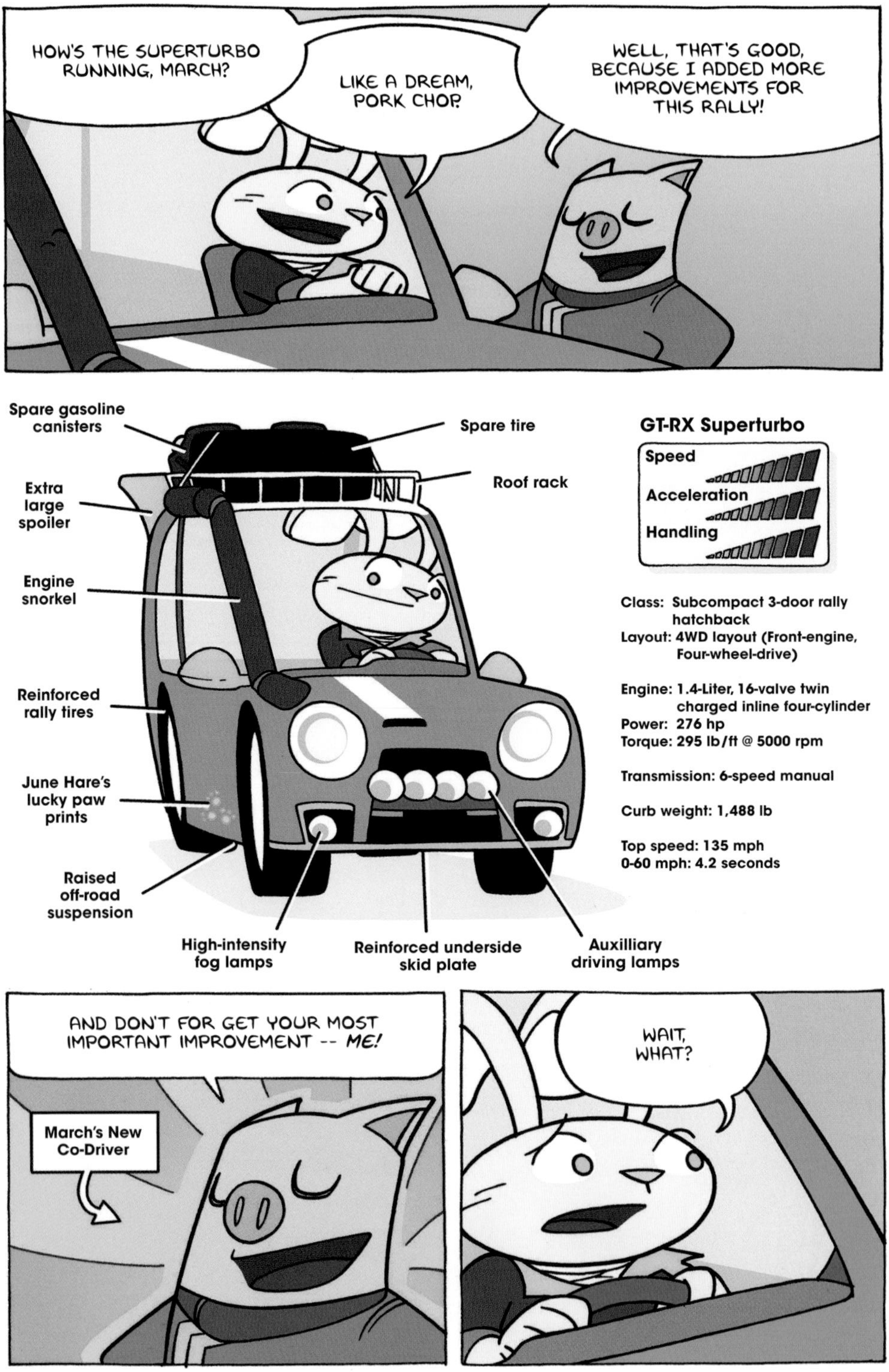
HOW'S THE SUPERTURBO RUNNING, MARCH?
LIKE A DREAM, PORK CHOP.
WELL, THAT'S GOOD, BECAUSE I ADDED MORE IMPROVEMENTS FOR THIS RALLY!
Spare gasoline canisters
Spare tire
Roof rack
Extra large spoiler
Engine snorkel
Reinforced rally tires
June Hare's lucky paw prints
Raised off-road suspension
High-intensity fog lamps
Reinforced underside skid plate
Auxilliary driving lamps
GT-RX Superturbo
Speed
Acceleration
Handling
Class: Subcompact 3-door rally hatchback
Layout: 4WD layout (Front-engine, Four-wheel-drive)
Engine: 1.4-Liter, 16-valve twin charged inline four-cylinder
Power: 276 hp
Torque: 295 lb/ft @ 5000 rpm
Transmission: 6-speed manual
Curb weight: 1,488 lb
Top speed: 135 mph
0-60 mph: 4.2 seconds
AND DON'T FOR GET YOUR MOST IMPORTANT IMPROVEMENT -- *ME!*
March's New Co-Driver
WAIT, WHAT?

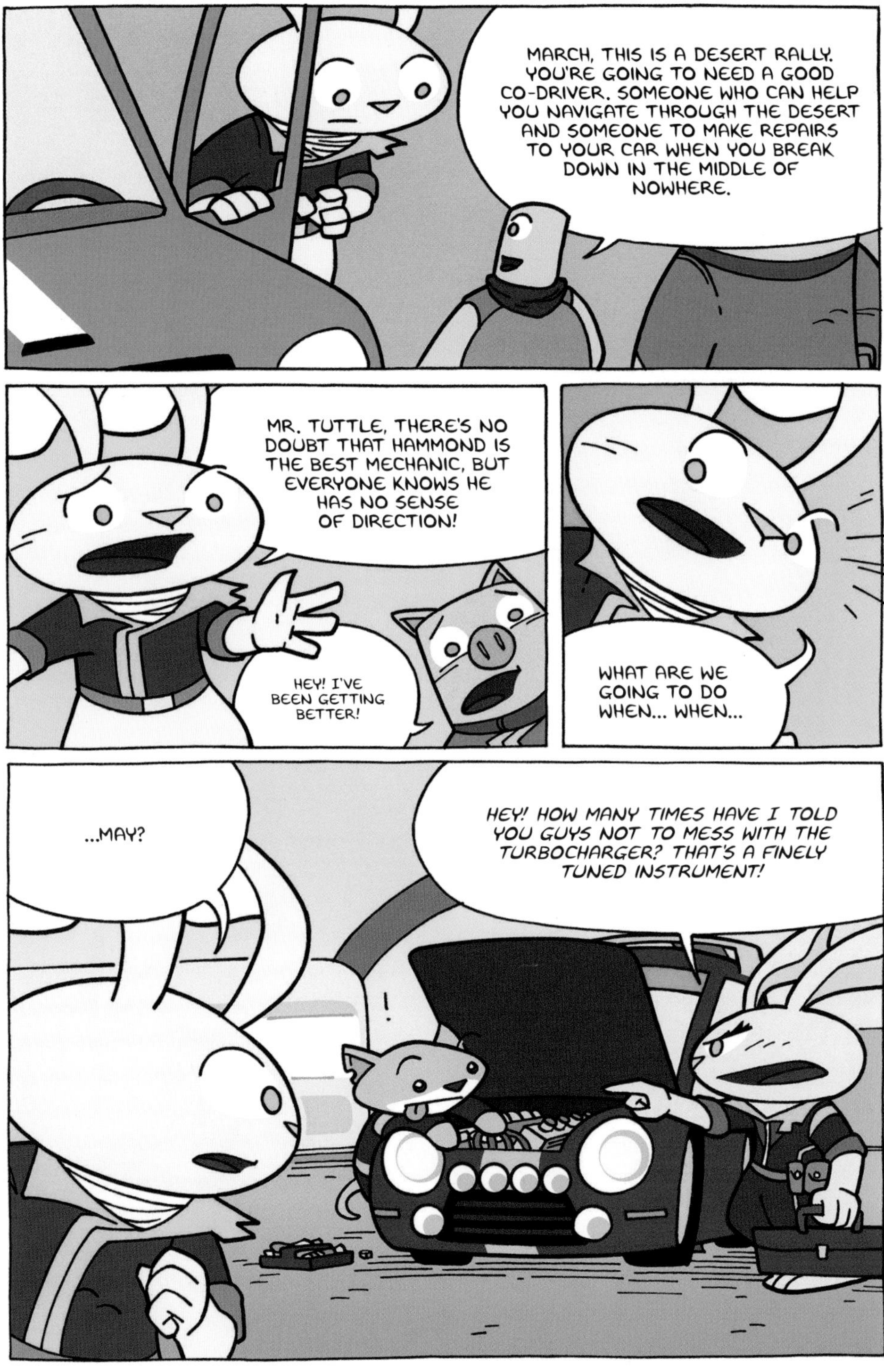
MARCH, THIS IS A DESERT RALLY. YOU'RE GOING TO NEED A GOOD CO-DRIVER. SOMEONE WHO CAN HELP YOU NAVIGATE THROUGH THE DESERT AND SOMEONE TO MAKE REPAIRS TO YOUR CAR WHEN YOU BREAK DOWN IN THE MIDDLE OF NOWHERE.
MR. TUTTLE, THERE'S NO DOUBT THAT HAMMOND IS THE BEST MECHANIC, BUT EVERYONE KNOWS HE HAS NO SENSE OF DIRECTION!
HEY! I'VE BEEN GETTING BETTER!
WHAT ARE WE GOING TO DO WHEN... WHEN...
...MAY?
!
HEY! HOW MANY TIMES HAVE I TOLD YOU GUYS NOT TO MESS WITH THE TURBOCHARGER? THAT'S A FINELY TUNED INSTRUMENT!

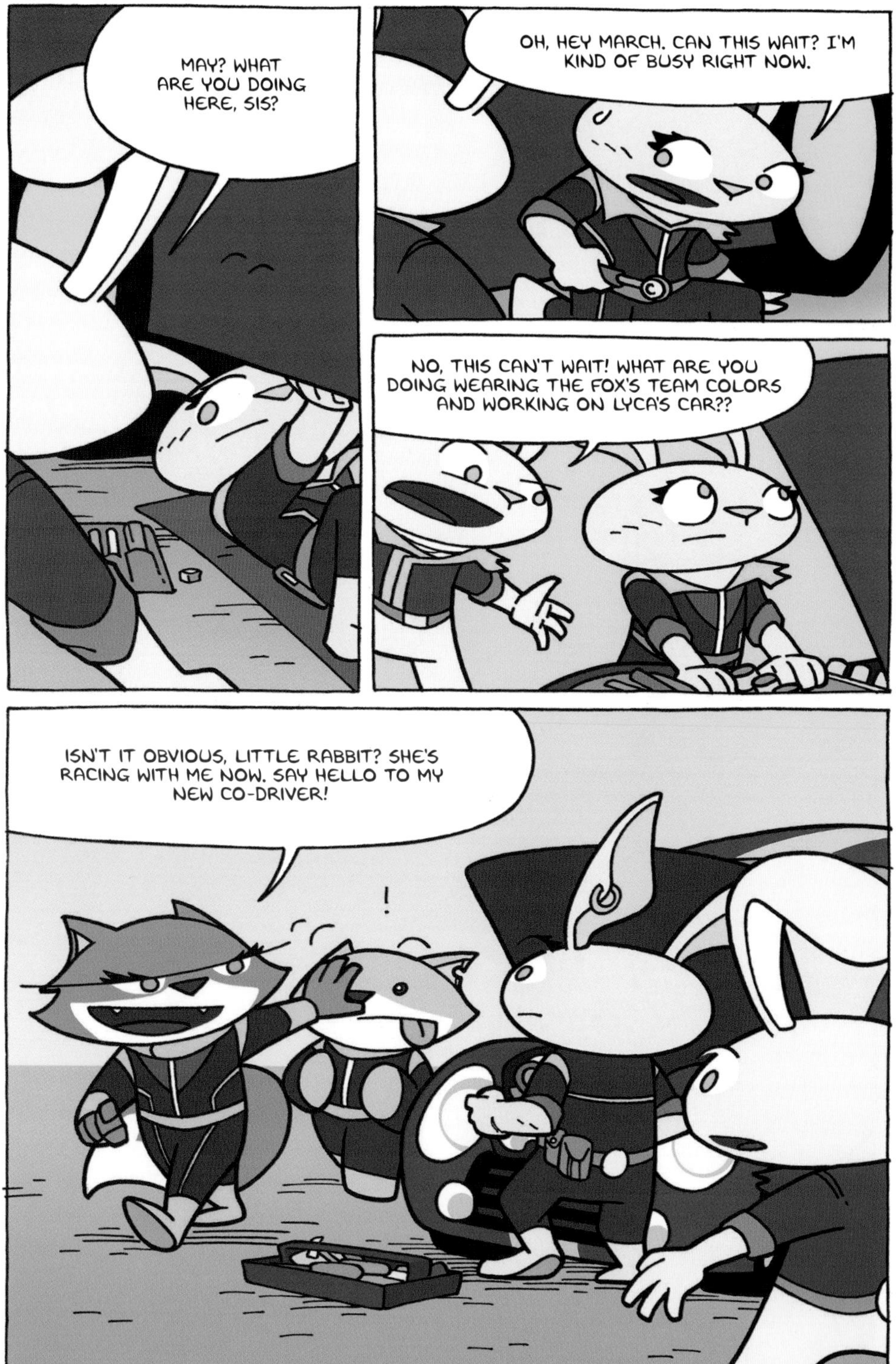
MAY? WHAT ARE YOU DOING HERE, SIS?
OH, HEY MARCH. CAN THIS WAIT? I'M KIND OF BUSY RIGHT NOW.
NO, THIS CAN'T WAIT! WHAT ARE YOU DOING WEARING THE FOX'S TEAM COLORS AND WORKING ON LYCA'S CAR??
ISN'T IT OBVIOUS, LITTLE RABBIT? SHE'S RACING WITH ME NOW. SAY HELLO TO MY NEW CO-DRIVER!
!

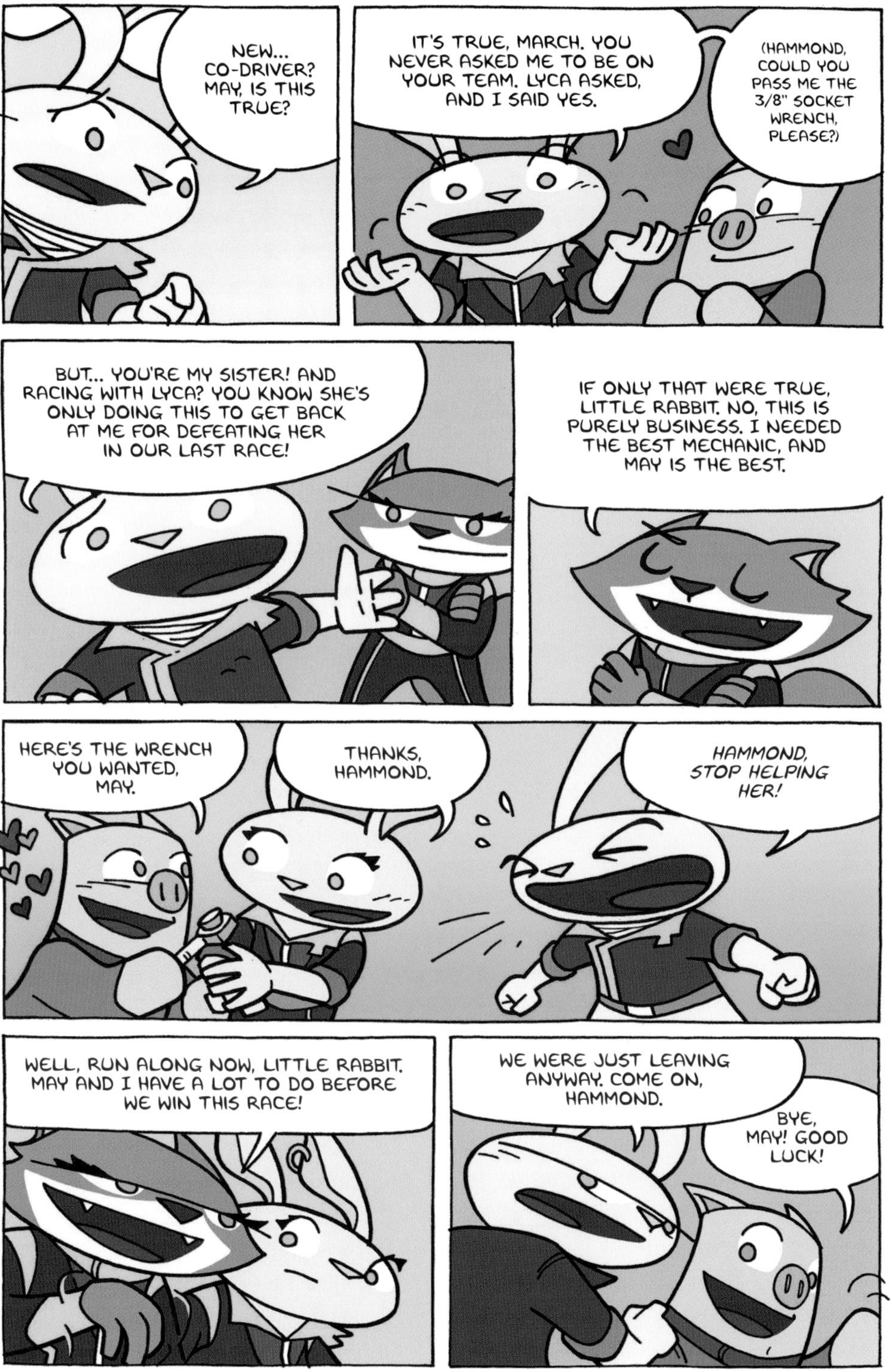
NEW... CO-DRIVER? MAY, IS THIS TRUE?
IT'S TRUE, MARCH. YOU NEVER ASKED ME TO BE ON YOUR TEAM. LYCA ASKED, AND I SAID YES.
(HAMMOND, COULD YOU PASS ME THE 3/8" SOCKET WRENCH, PLEASE?)
BUT... YOU'RE MY SISTER! AND RACING WITH LYCA? YOU KNOW SHE'S ONLY DOING THIS TO GET BACK AT ME FOR DEFEATING HER IN OUR LAST RACE!
IF ONLY THAT WERE TRUE, LITTLE RABBIT. NO, THIS IS PURELY BUSINESS. I NEEDED THE BEST MECHANIC, AND MAY IS THE BEST.
HERE'S THE WRENCH YOU WANTED, MAY.
THANKS, HAMMOND.
HAMMOND, STOP HELPING HER!
WELL, RUN ALONG NOW, LITTLE RABBIT. MAY AND I HAVE A LOT TO DO BEFORE WE WIN THIS RACE!
WE WERE JUST LEAVING ANYWAY. COME ON, HAMMOND.
BYE, MAY! GOOD LUCK!

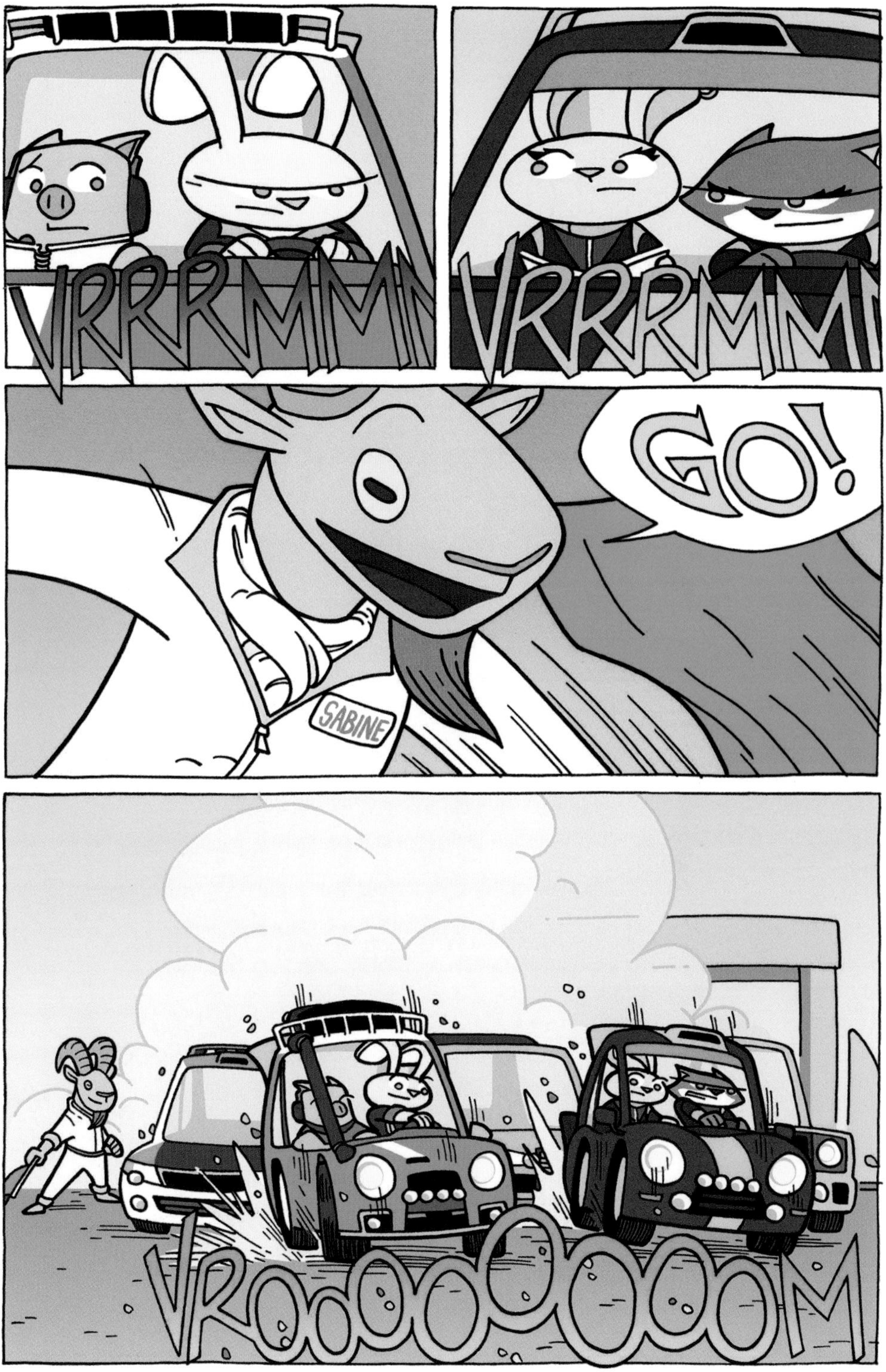
VRRRMMM
VRRRMMM
GO!
SABINE
VROOOOOOOOOM

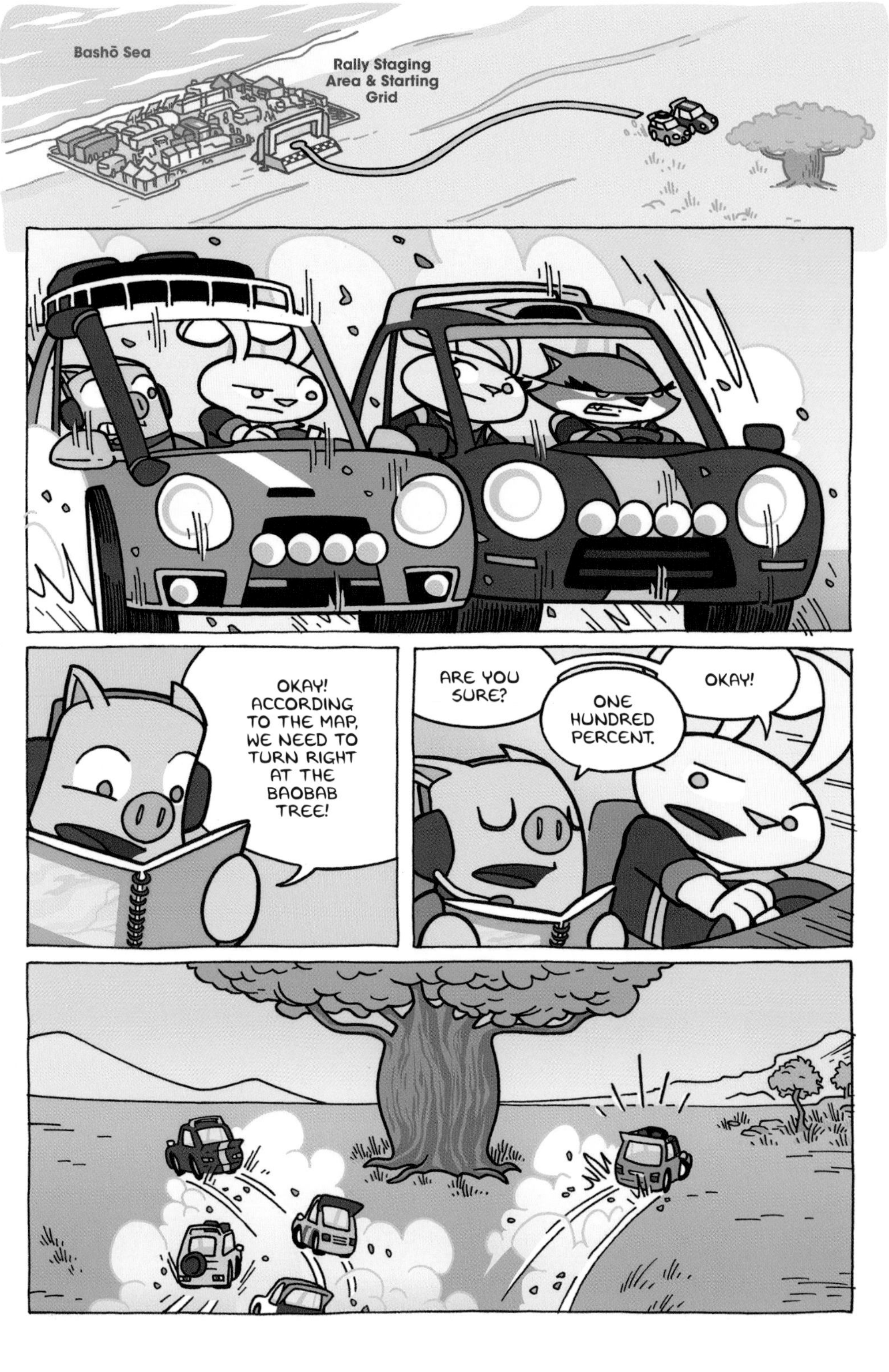
Bashō Sea
Rally Staging Area & Starting Grid
OKAY! ACCORDING TO THE MAP, WE NEED TO TURN RIGHT AT THE BAOBAB TREE!
ARE YOU SURE?
ONE HUNDRED PERCENT.
OKAY!

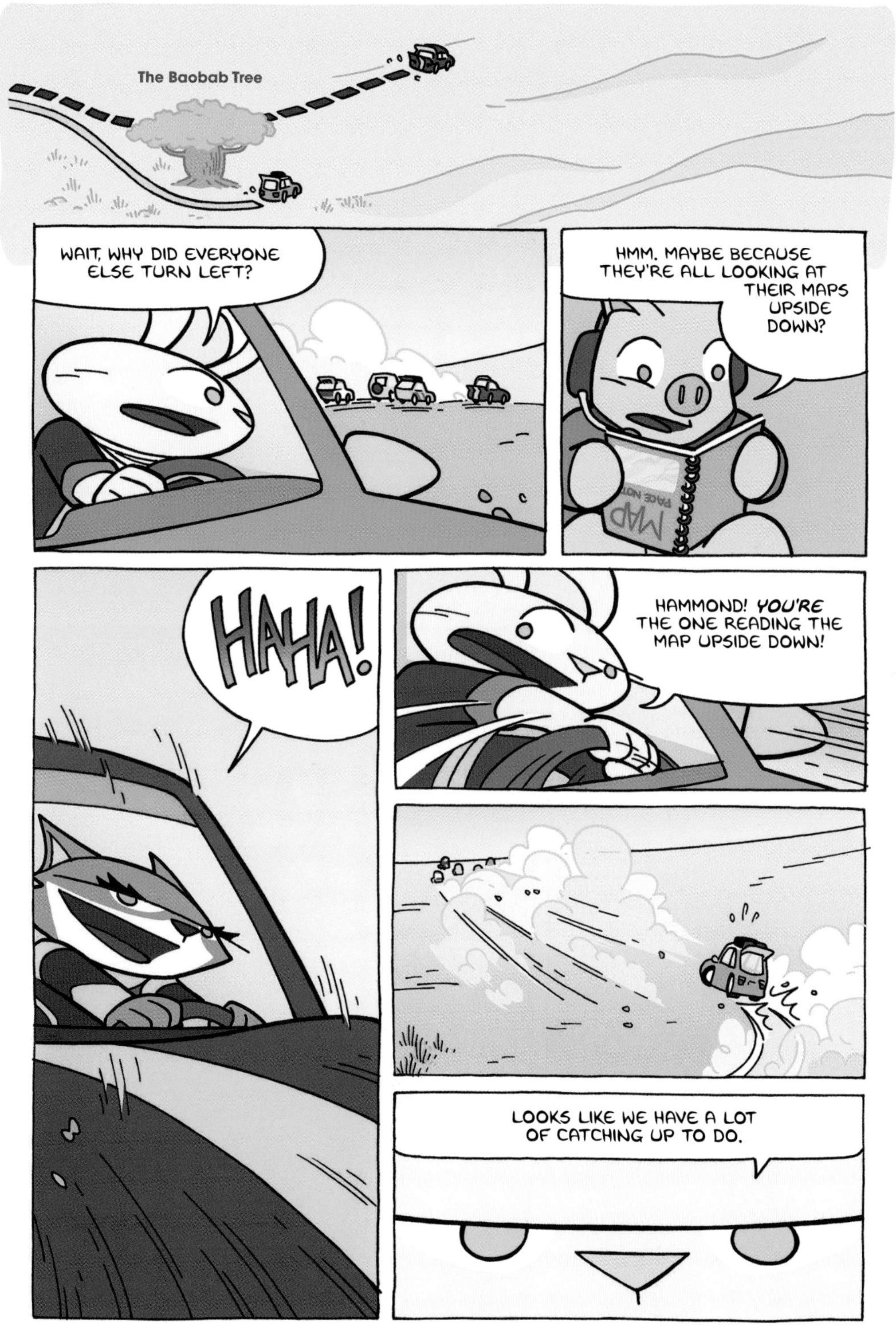
The Baobab Tree
WAIT, WHY DID EVERYONE ELSE TURN LEFT?
HMM. MAYBE BECAUSE THEY'RE ALL LOOKING AT THEIR MAPS UPSIDE DOWN?
MAP
PACE NOTES
HAHA!
HAMMOND! *YOU'RE* THE ONE READING THE MAP UPSIDE DOWN!
LOOKS LIKE WE HAVE A LOT OF CATCHING UP TO DO.

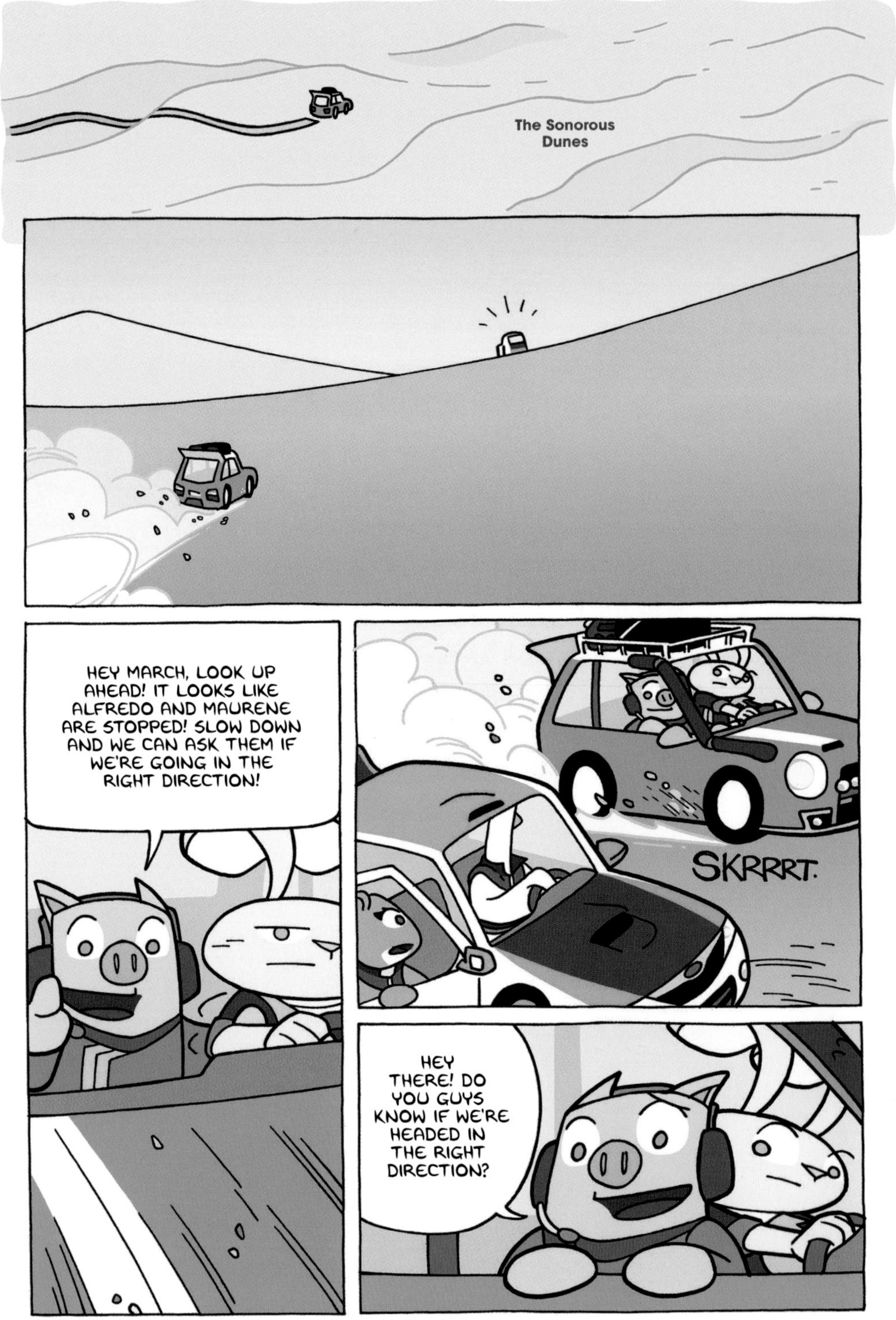
The Sonorous Dunes
HEY MARCH, LOOK UP AHEAD! IT LOOKS LIKE ALFREDO AND MAURENE ARE STOPPED! SLOW DOWN AND WE CAN ASK THEM IF WE'RE GOING IN THE RIGHT DIRECTION!
SKRRRT.
HEY THERE! DO YOU GUYS KNOW IF WE'RE HEADED IN THE RIGHT DIRECTION?

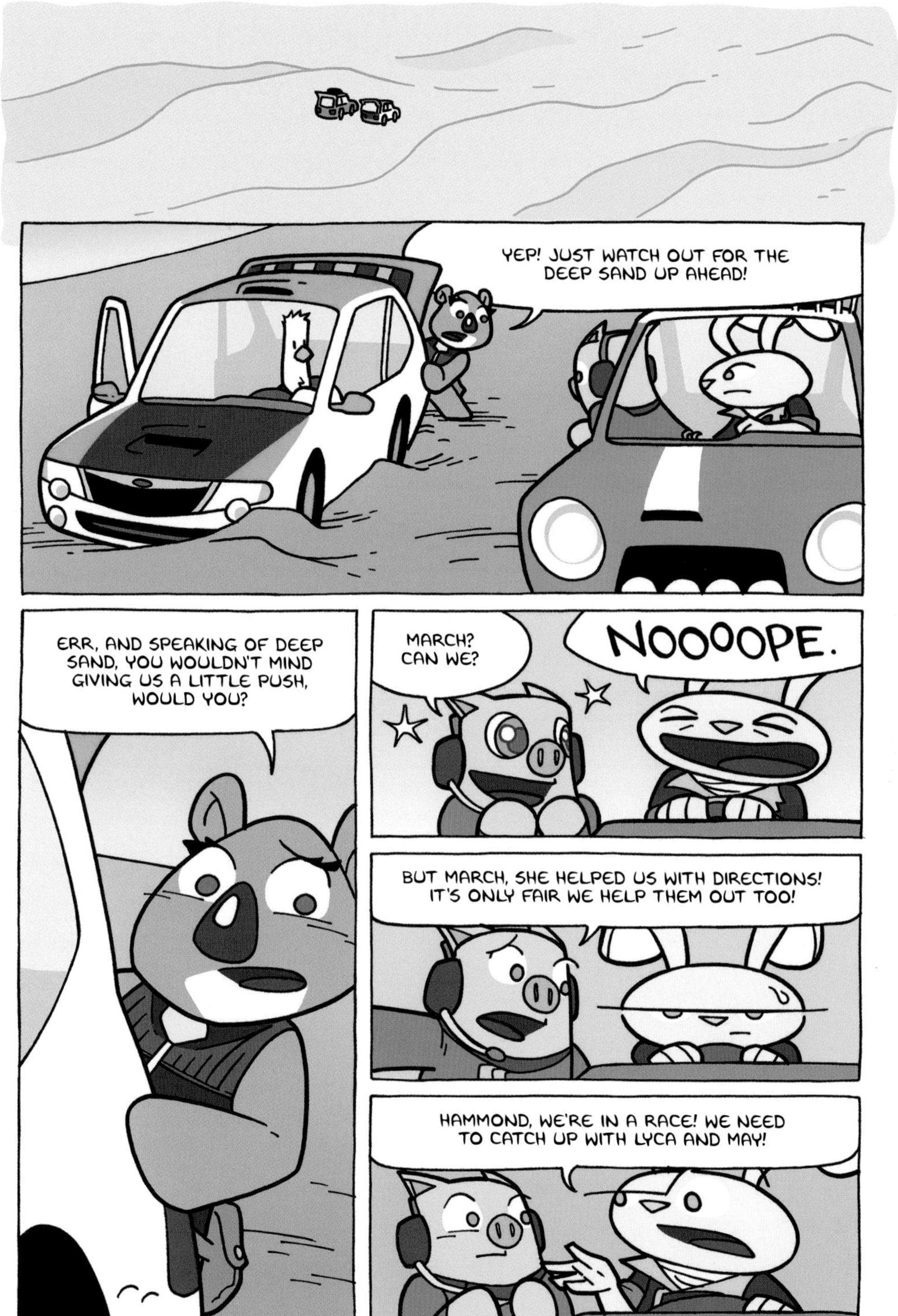
YEP! JUST WATCH OUT FOR THE DEEP SAND UP AHEAD!
ERR, AND SPEAKING OF DEEP SAND, YOU WOULDN'T MIND GIVING US A LITTLE PUSH, WOULD YOU?
MARCH? CAN WE?
NOOOOPE.
BUT MARCH, SHE HELPED US WITH DIRECTIONS! IT'S ONLY FAIR WE HELP THEM OUT TOO!
HAMMOND, WE'RE IN A RACE! WE NEED TO CATCH UP WITH LYCA AND MAY!

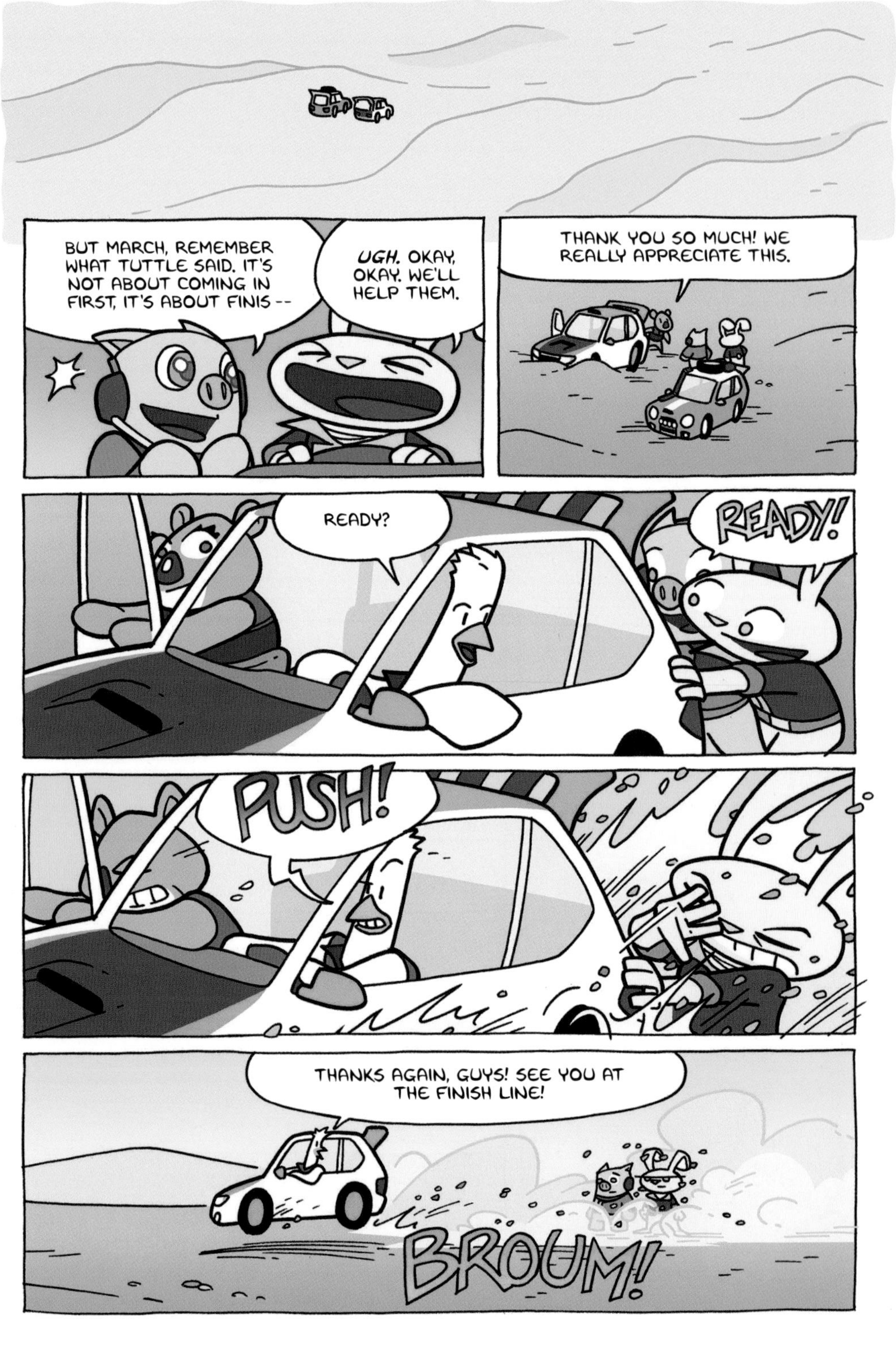

BUT MARCH, REMEMBER WHAT TUTTLE SAID. IT'S NOT ABOUT COMING IN FIRST, IT'S ABOUT FINIS --
UGH. OKAY, OKAY. WE'LL HELP THEM.
THANK YOU SO MUCH! WE REALLY APPRECIATE THIS.
READY?
READY!
PUSH!
THANKS AGAIN, GUYS! SEE YOU AT THE FINISH LINE!
BROUM!

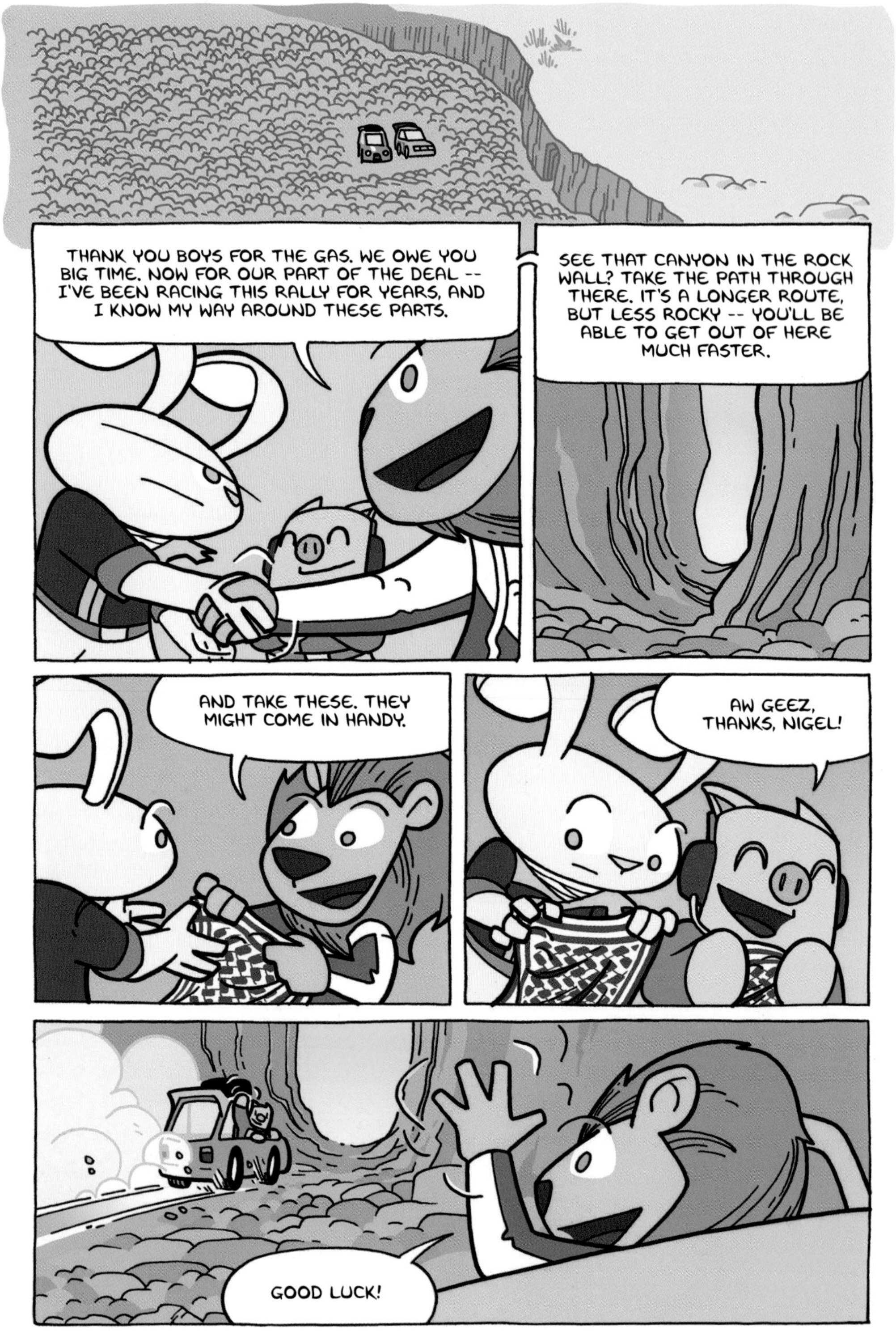
THANK YOU BOYS FOR THE GAS. WE OWE YOU BIG TIME. NOW FOR OUR PART OF THE DEAL -- I'VE BEEN RACING THIS RALLY FOR YEARS, AND I KNOW MY WAY AROUND THESE PARTS.
SEE THAT CANYON IN THE ROCK WALL? TAKE THE PATH THROUGH THERE. IT'S A LONGER ROUTE, BUT LESS ROCKY -- YOU'LL BE ABLE TO GET OUT OF HERE MUCH FASTER.
AND TAKE THESE. THEY MIGHT COME IN HANDY.
AW GEEZ, THANKS, NIGEL!
GOOD LUCK!

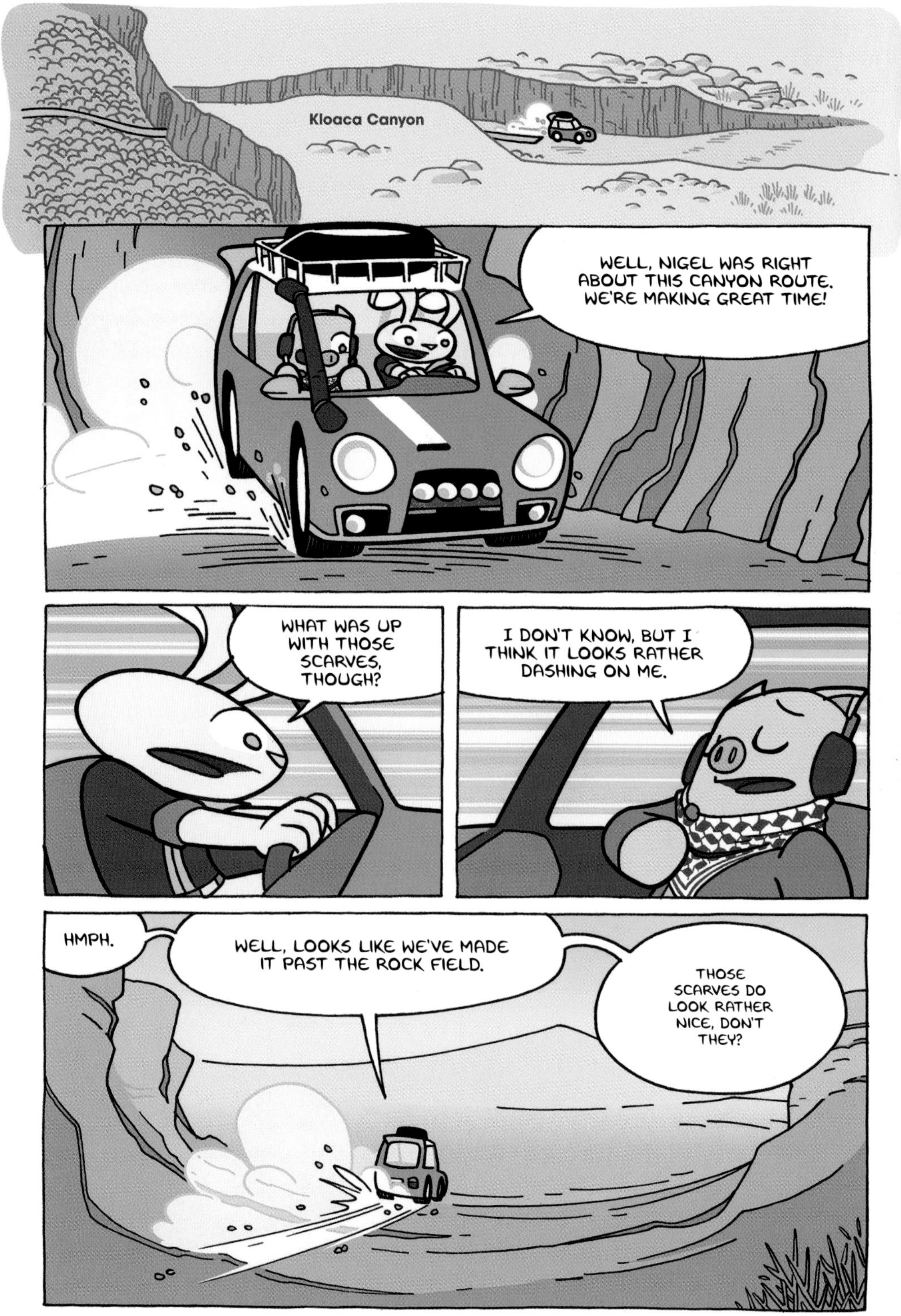
Kloaca Canyon
WELL, NIGEL WAS RIGHT ABOUT THIS CANYON ROUTE. WE'RE MAKING GREAT TIME!
WHAT WAS UP WITH THOSE SCARVES, THOUGH?
I DON'T KNOW, BUT I THINK IT LOOKS RATHER DASHING ON ME.
HMPH.
WELL, LOOKS LIKE WE'VE MADE IT PAST THE ROCK FIELD.
THOSE SCARVES DO LOOK RATHER NICE, DON'T THEY?

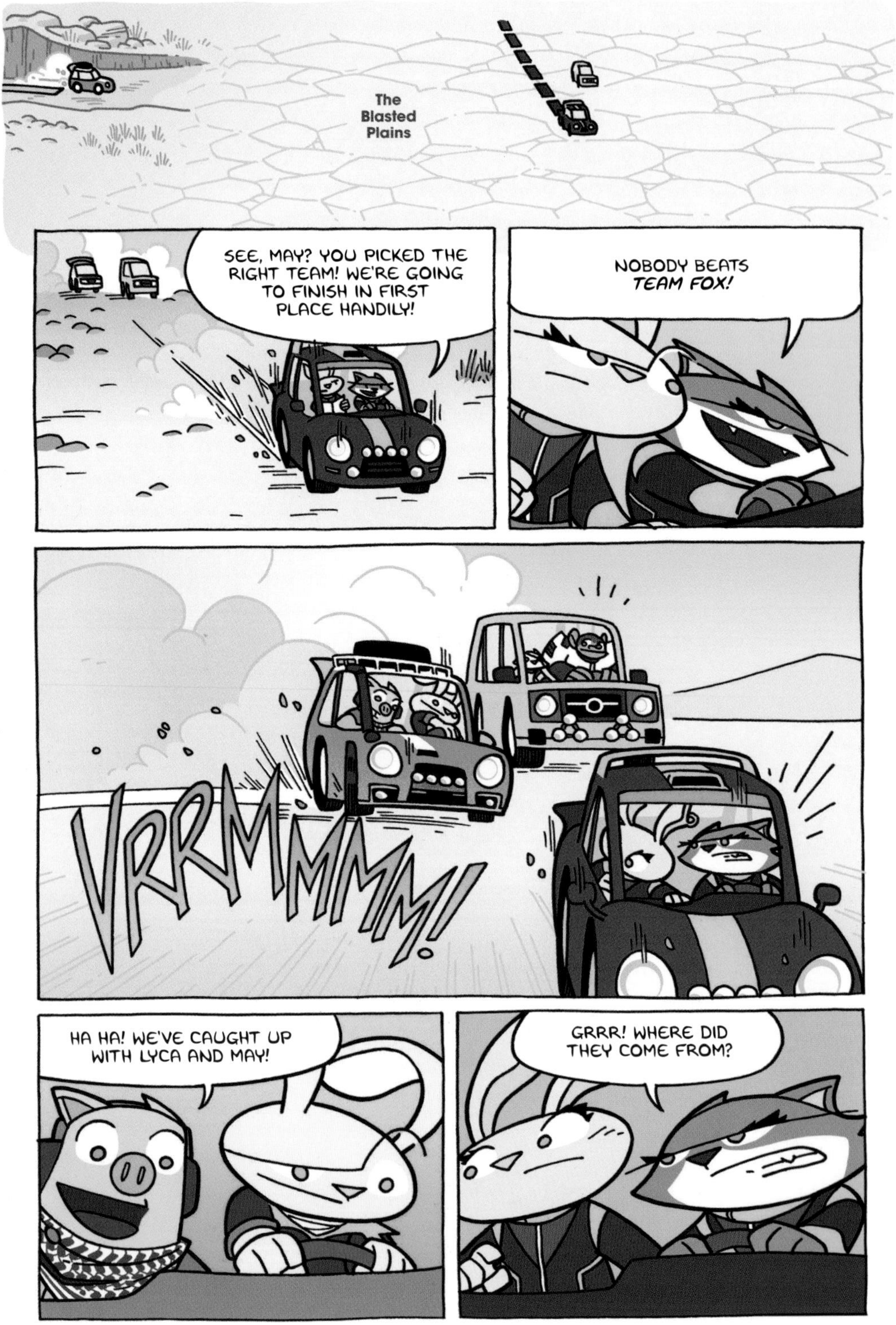
The Blasted Plains
SEE, MAY? YOU PICKED THE RIGHT TEAM! WE'RE GOING TO FINISH IN FIRST PLACE HANDILY!
NOBODY BEATS *TEAM FOX!*
VRRMMMM!
HA HA! WE'VE CAUGHT UP WITH LYCA AND MAY!
GRRR! WHERE DID THEY COME FROM?

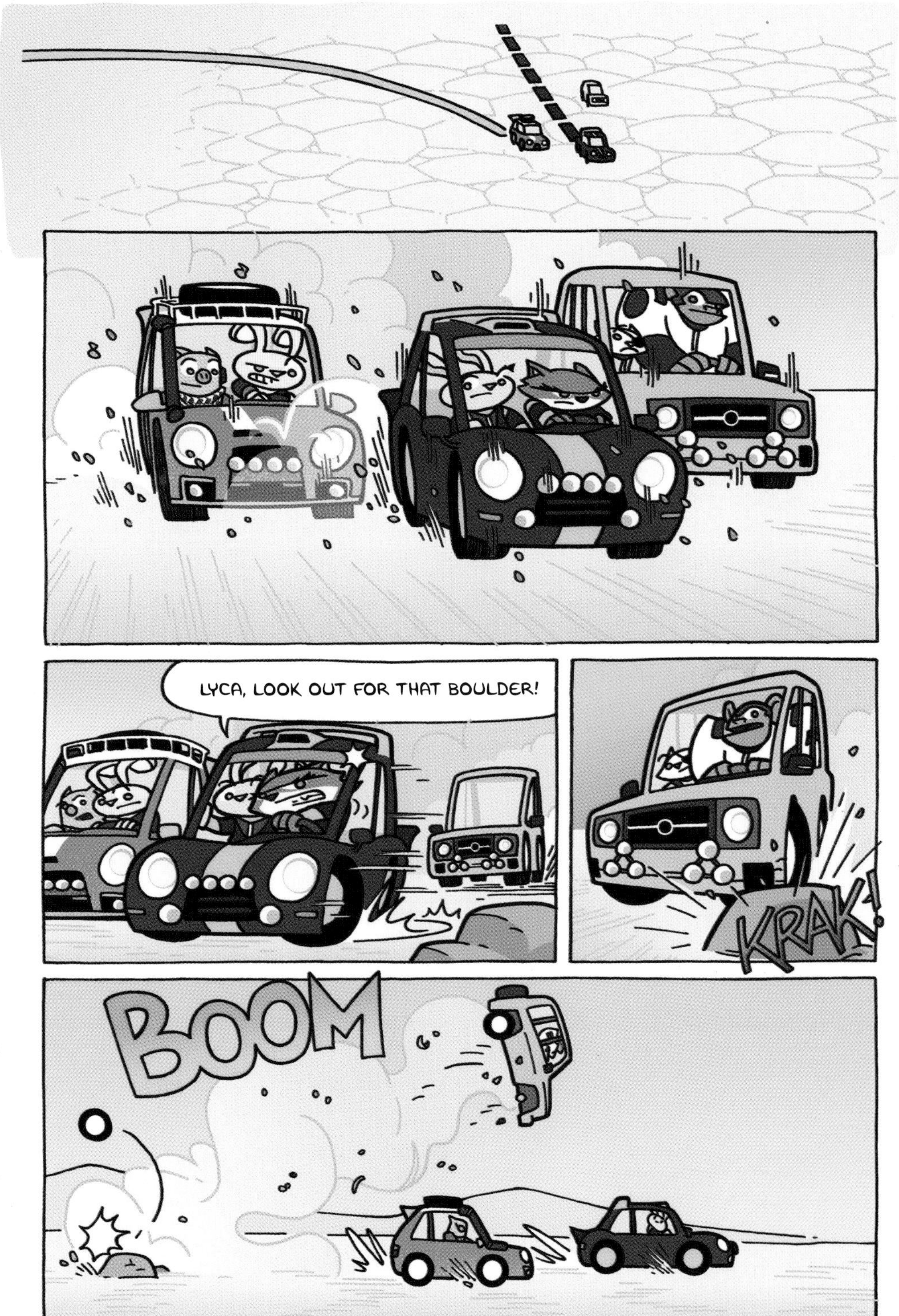
LYCA, LOOK OUT FOR THAT BOULDER!
KRAK!
BOOM

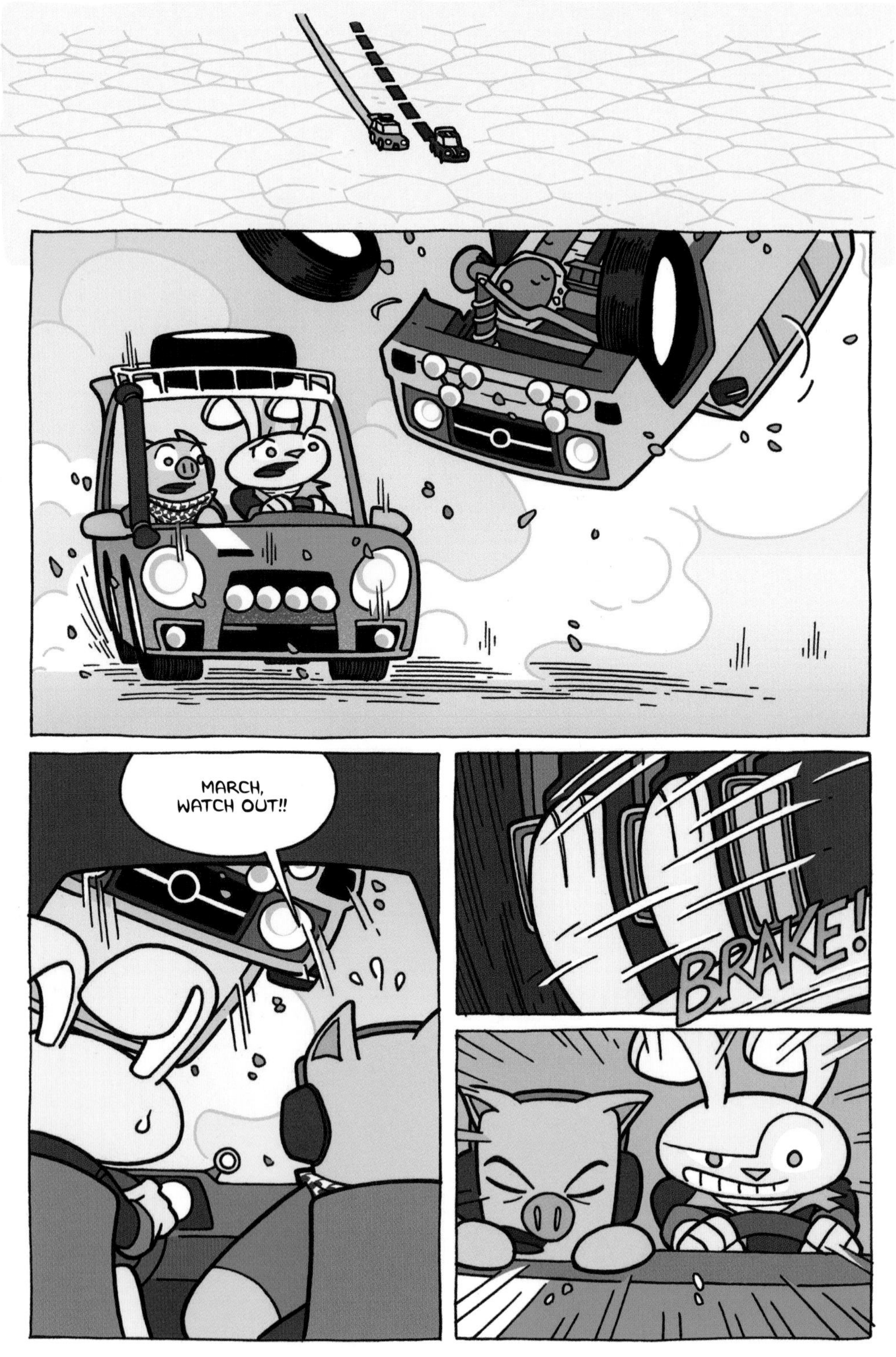
MARCH,
WATCH OUT!!
BRAKE!

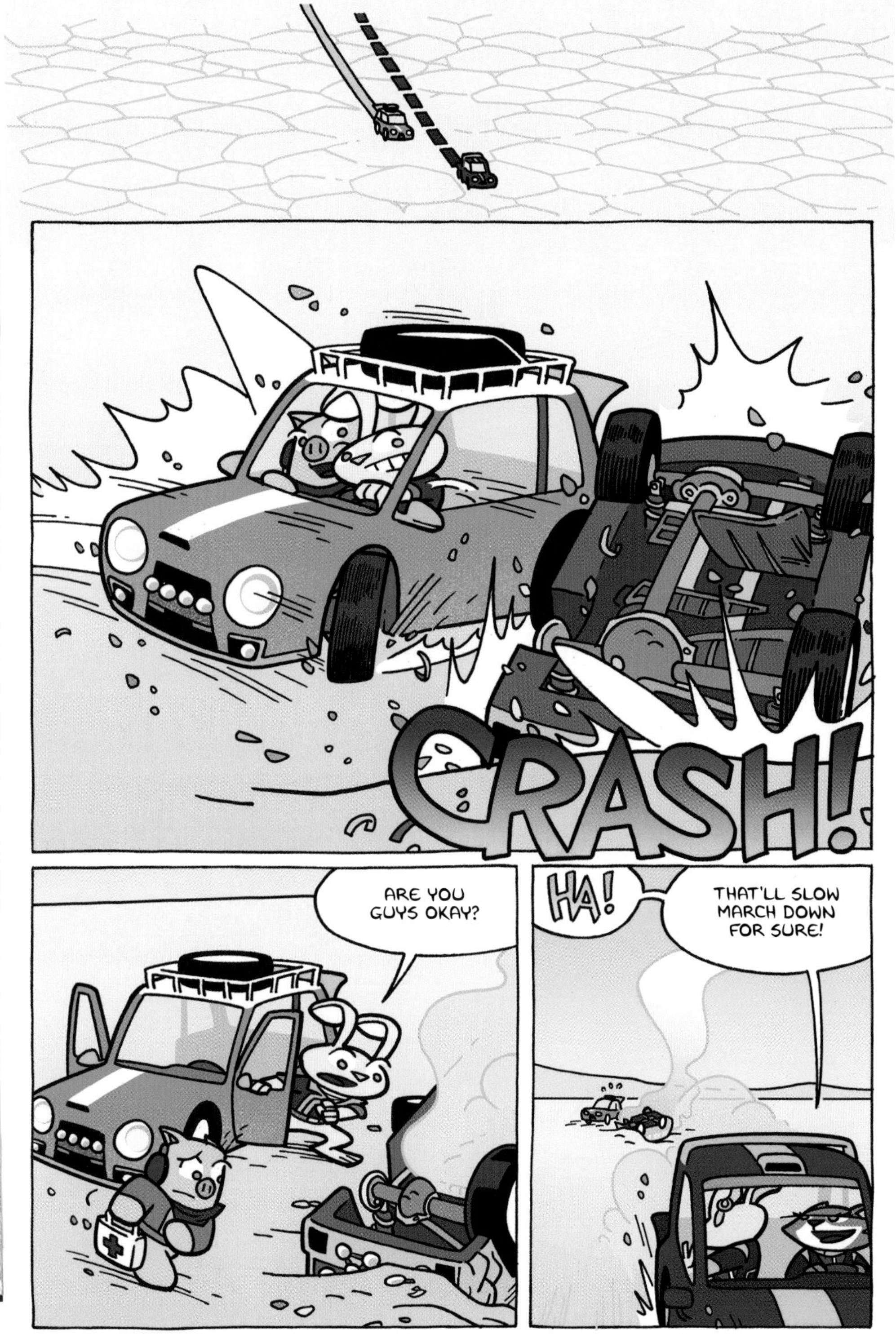
CRASH!
ARE YOU GUYS OKAY?
HA!
THAT'LL SLOW MARCH DOWN FOR SURE!

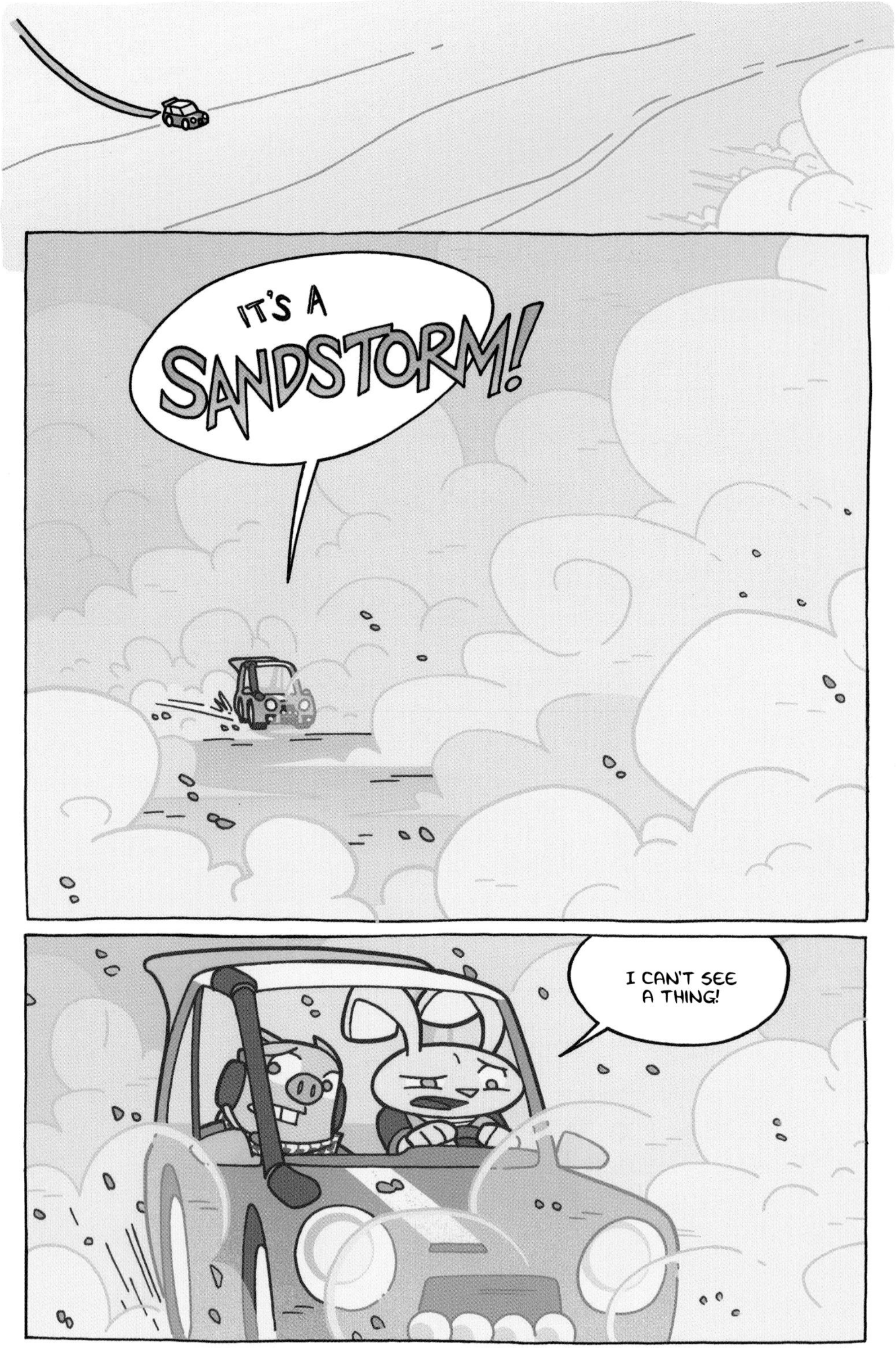
IT'S A SANDSTORM!
I CAN'T SEE A THING!

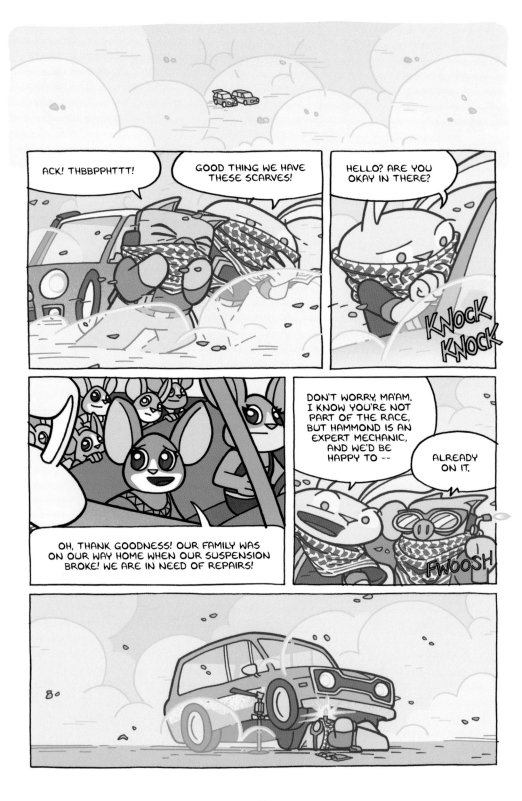

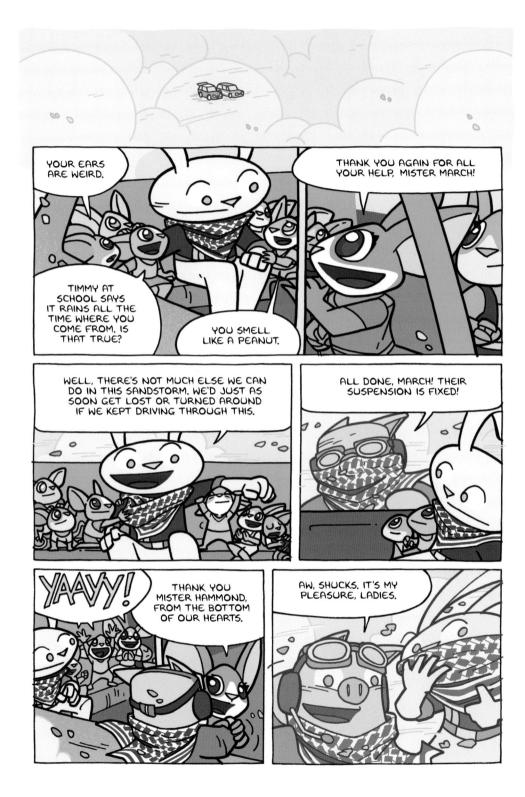

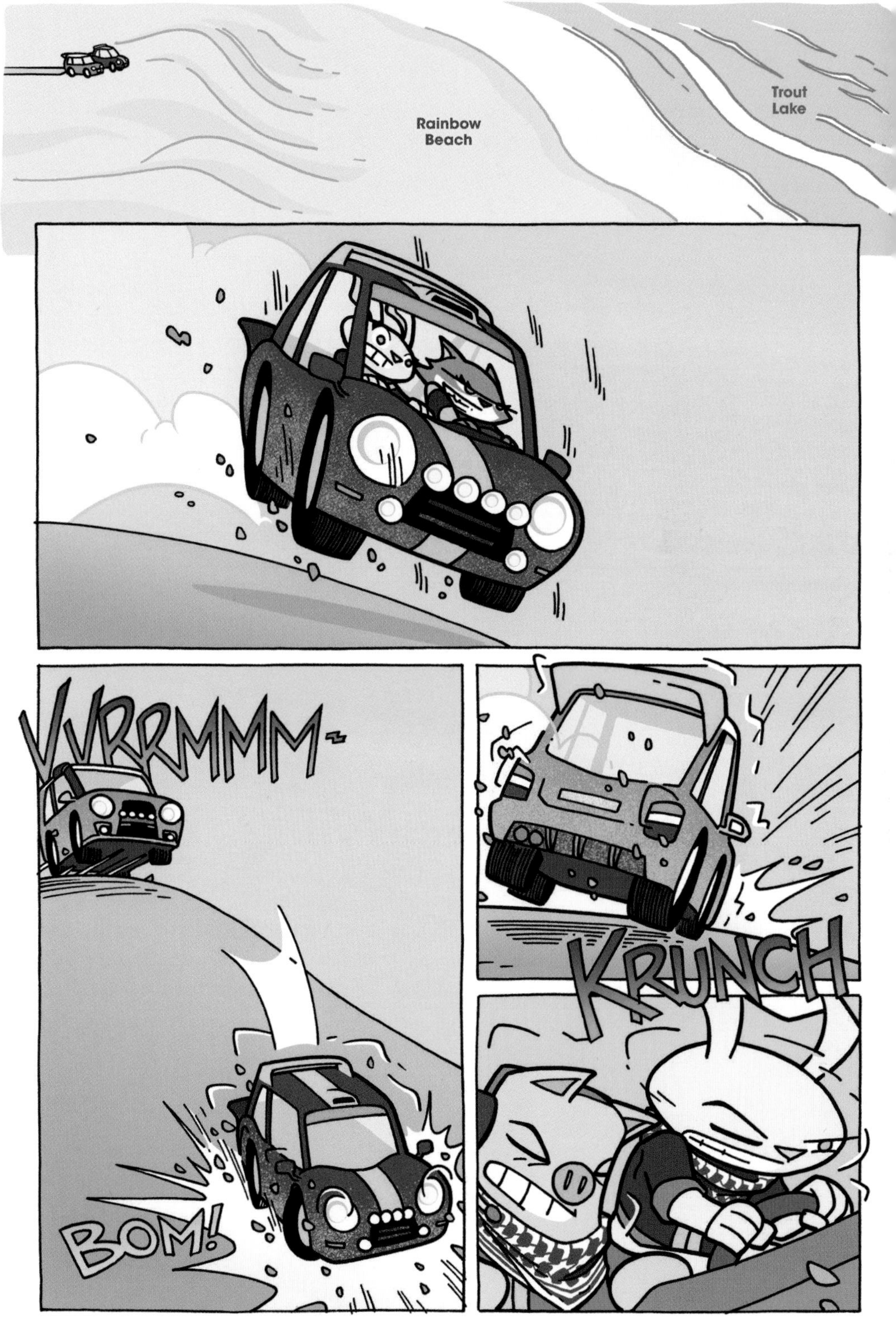
Rainbow Beach
Trout Lake
VVRRMMM
BOM!
KRUNCH

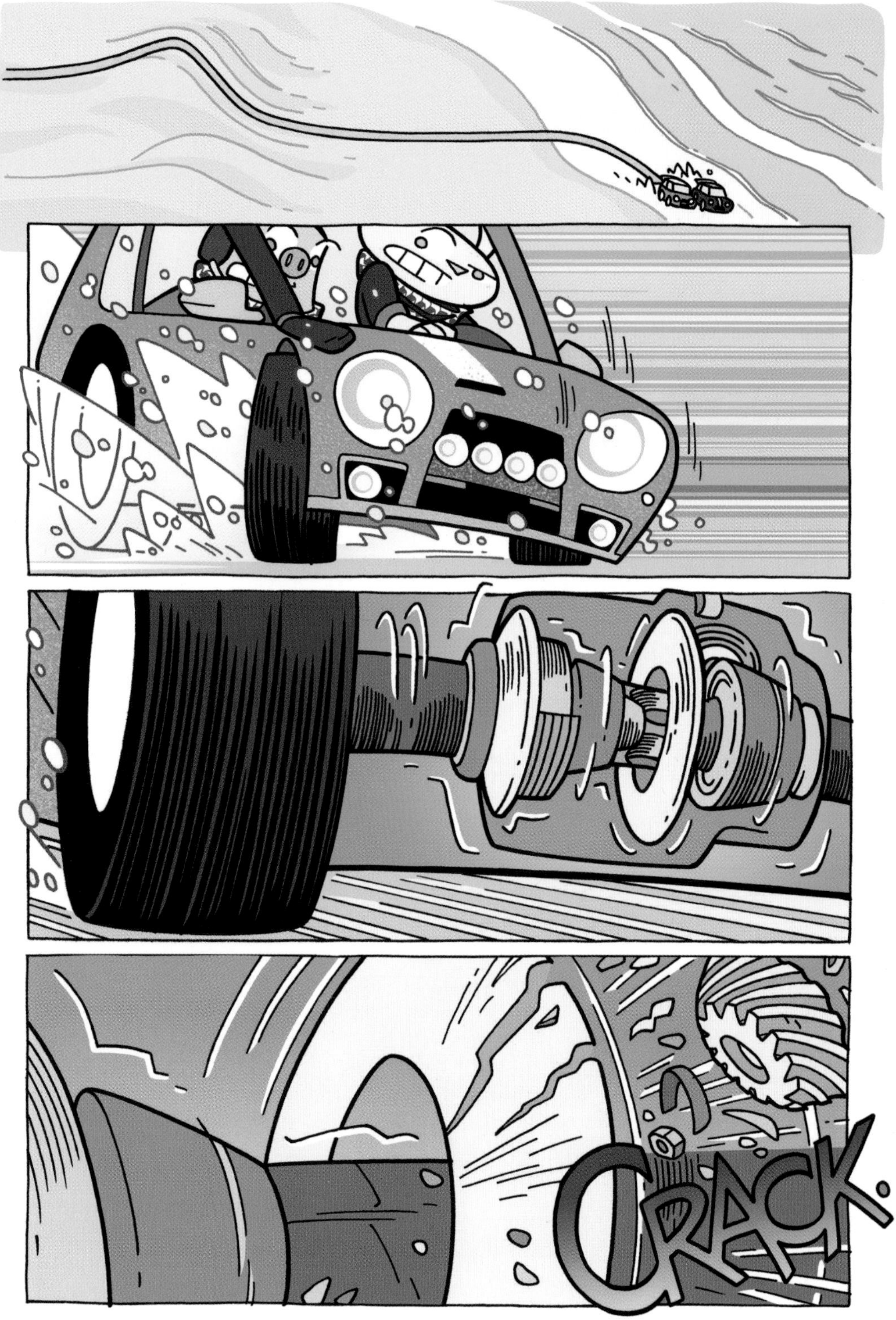
CRACK

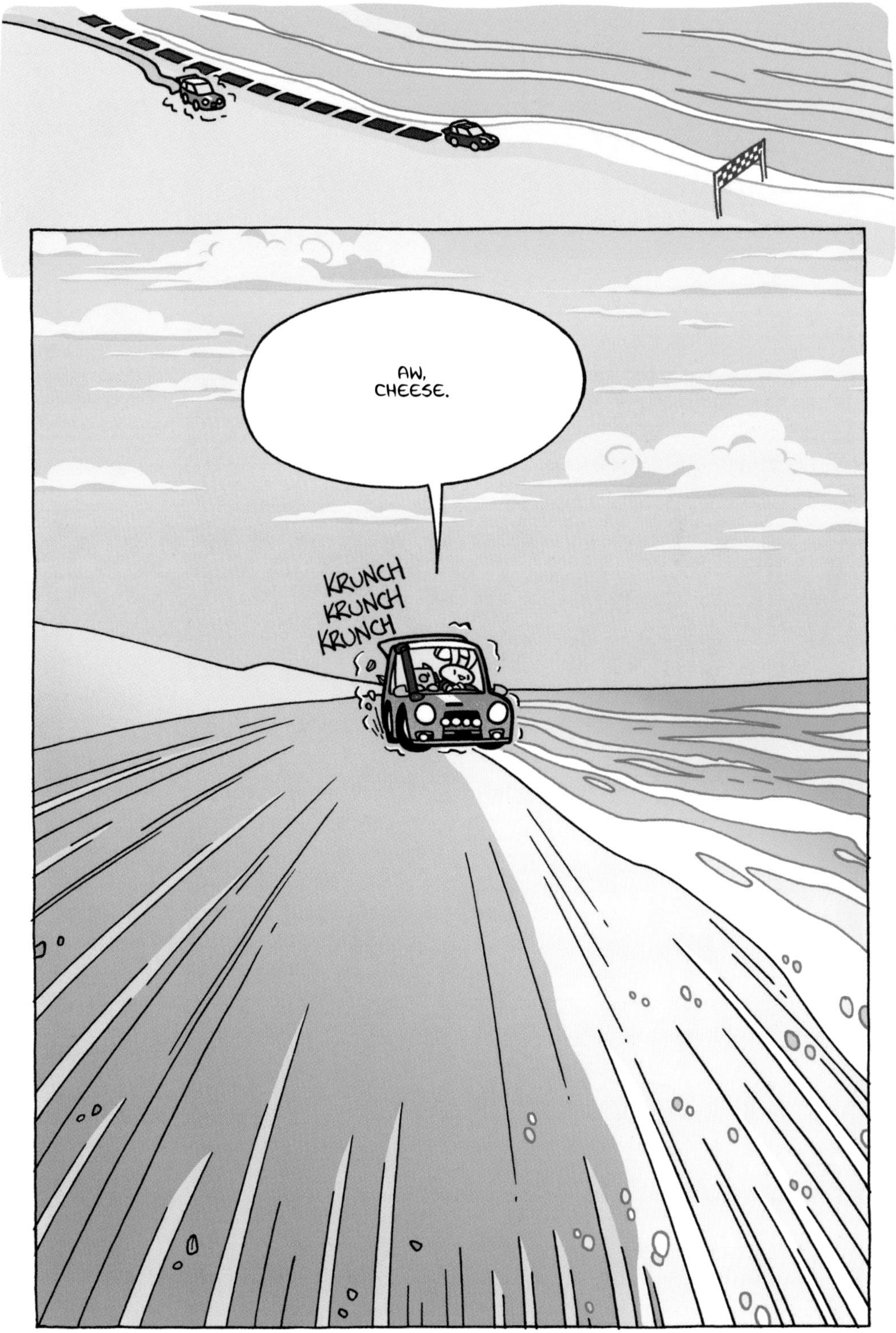
AW, CHEESE.
KRUNCH
KRUNCH
KRUNCH

40

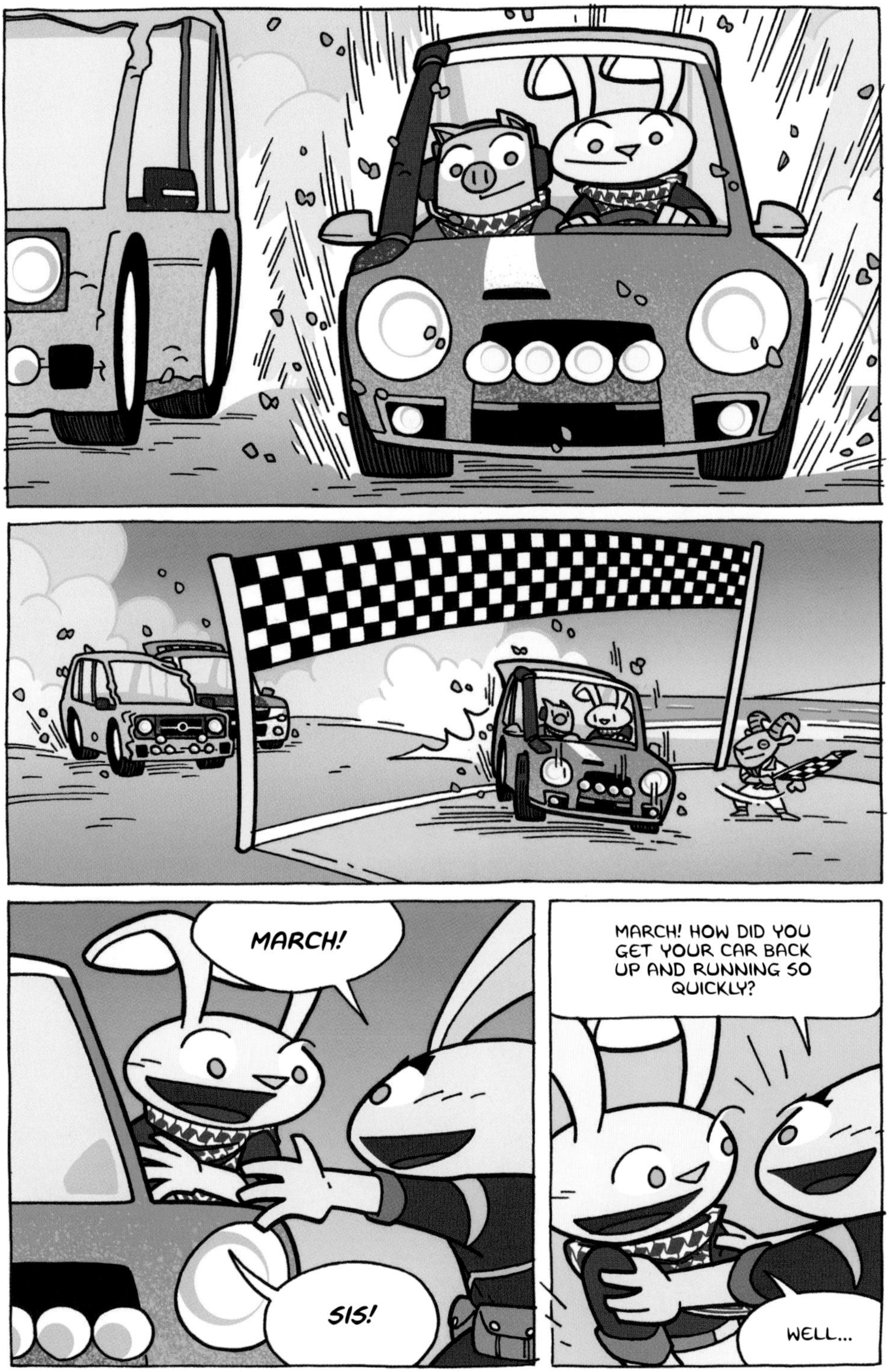
MARCH!
SIS!
MARCH! HOW DID YOU GET YOUR CAR BACK UP AND RUNNING SO QUICKLY?
WELL...

44

SKETCHES

MARCH + HAMMOND IN THEIR YOUTH

Very early design sketches of March and Hammond

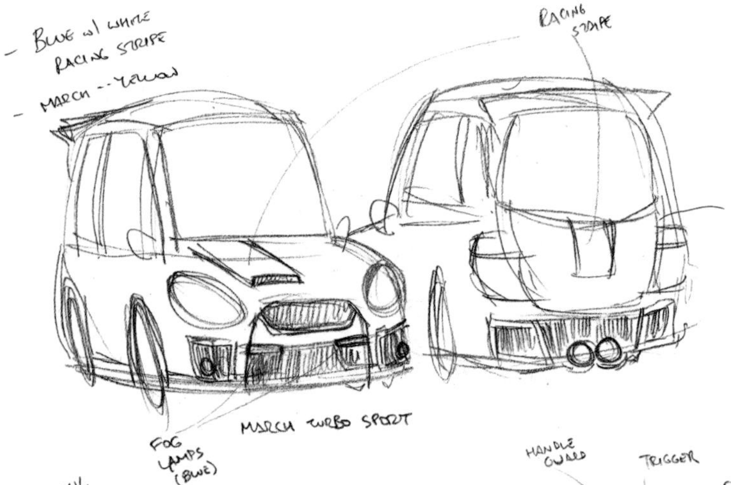

- BLUE w/ WHITE RACING STRIPE
- MARCH -- YELLOW

RACING STRIPE

Early design sketches of March and Lyca's cars

MARCH TURBO SPORT

FOG LAMPS (BLUE)

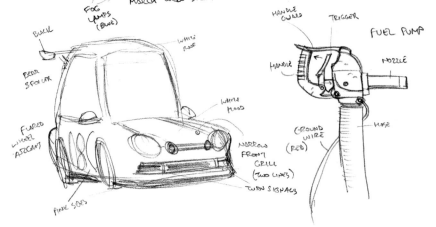

BLACK

REAR SPOILER

WHITE ROOF

FLARED WHEEL ARCHES

WHITE HOOD

PINK SIDES

NARROW FRONT GRILL (TWO LIGHTS)

TWIN SIGNALS

HANDLE GUARD   TRIGGER

FUEL PUMP

HANDLE

NOZZLE

GROUND WIRE (RED)

HOSE

New vehicle concepts

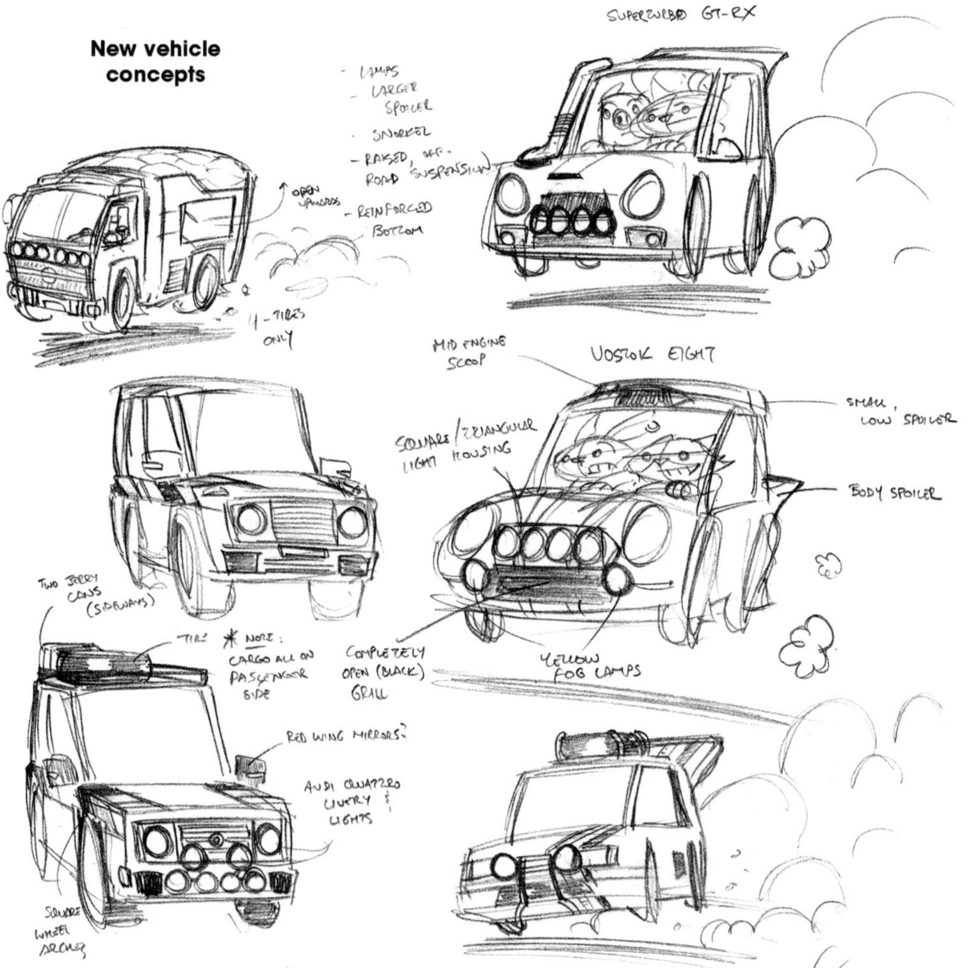
SUPERTURBO GT-RX
- LAMPS
- LARGER SPOILER
- SNORKEL
- RAISED, OFF-ROAD SUSPENSION
- REINFORCED BOTTOM
OPEN UPWARDS
4-TIRES ONLY
MID ENGINE SCOOP
VOSTOK EIGHT
SMALL, LOW SPOILER
SQUARE/TRIANGULAR LIGHT HOUSING
BODY SPOILER
TWO JERRY CANS (SIDEWAYS)
TIRE
* NOTE: CARGO ALL ON PASSENGER SIDE
COMPLETELY OPEN (BLACK) GRILL
YELLOW FOG LAMPS
RED WING MIRRORS?
AUDI QUATTRO LIVERY & LIGHTS
SQUARE WHEEL ARCHES

New character design sketches

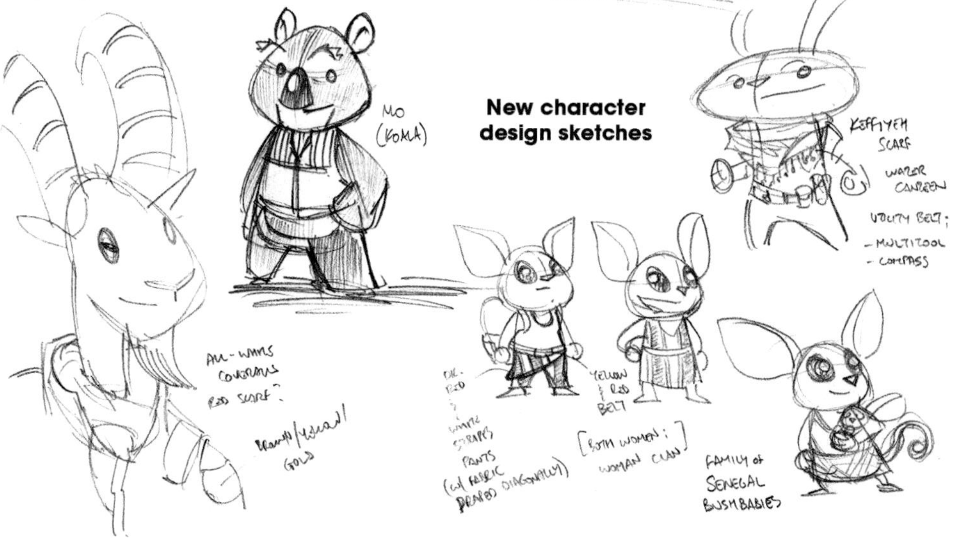
MO (KOALA)
KEFFIYEH SCARF
WATER CANTEEN
UTILITY BELT; - MULTITOOL - COMPASS
ALL-WEATHER COVERALLS
RED SCARF?
BROWN/YELLOW/GOLD
OR-RED & WHITE STRIPES PANTS (W/ FABRIC DRAPED DIAGONALLY)
YELLOW & RED BELT
[BOTH WOMEN; WOMAN CLAN]
FAMILY of SENEGAL BUSHBABIES

KEAN SOO

Kean Soo was born in the United Kingdom, grew up in various parts of Canada and Hong Kong, trained as an electrical engineer, and now draws comics for a living. A former assistant editor and contributor for the FLIGHT comics anthology, Kean also created the award-winning Jellaby series of graphic novels.

Kean's first date with his wife was a month-long drive across Italy and the South of France in a Fiat 500.

Kean would also like to thank Judy Hansen, Donnie Lemke, Brann Garvey, Tony Cliff, Kazu Kibuishi, everyone in the FLIGHT crew, and Tory Woollcott for making March Grand Prix such a joy to work on.

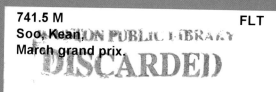